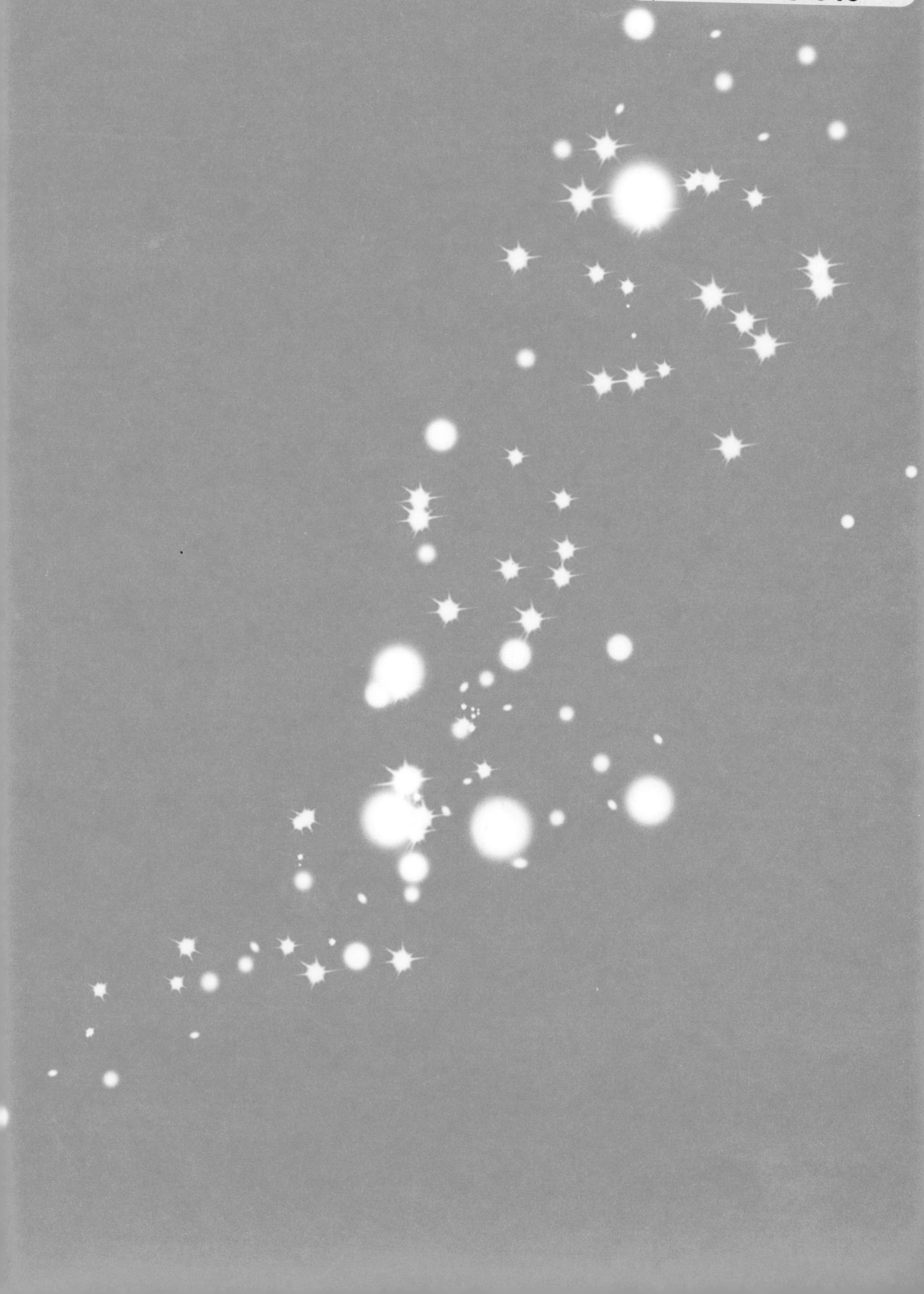

5

"The Dragon's Dance"

MICHEL RODRIGUE • Writer

ANTONELLO DALENA & MANUELA RAZZI • Artists

CECILIA GIUMENTO • Colorist

New York

GRAPHIC NOVELS AVAILABLE FROM PAPERCUTZ

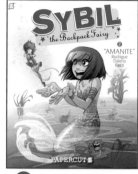

1 "NINA"

2 "AMANITE"

3 "AITHOR"

4 "PRINCESS NINA"

5 "THE DRAGON'S DANCE"

SYBIL THE BACKPACK FAIRY graphic novels are available in hardcover for $10.99 each, except #2, for $11.99 from book-sellers everywhere. Order online at papercutz.com. Order by mail: please add $4.00 for postage and handling for first book ordered, and add $1.00 for each additional book. Please make check payable to NBM Publishing. Send to: Papercutz, 160 Broadway, Suite 700, East Wing, New York, NY 10038 or call 800 866 1223 (9-6 EST M-F) MC, Visa, AmEx accepted.

Sybil the Backpack Fairy
#5 "The Dragon's Dance"
MICHEL RODRIGUE – Writer
ANTONELLO DALENA & MANUELA RAZZI – Artists
CECILIA GIUMENTO – Colorist
JOE JOHNSON – Translation
TOM ORZECHOWSKI – Lettering
JEFF WHITMAN – Production Coordinator
BETH SCORZATO – Editor
MICHAEL PETRANEK – Associate Editor

JIM SALICRUP
Editor-in-Chief

© EDITIONS DU LOMBARD (DARGAUD-LOMBARD S.A.)
2014 by Rodrigue, Dalena, Razzi.
www.lombard.com All rights reserved.
English translation and other
editorial matter copyright © 2015 by Papercutz.
ISBN: 978-1-62991-171-7

Printed in China
March 2015 by O.G. Printing Productions, LTD.
Units 2 & 3, 5/F Lemmi Centre
50 Hoi Yuen Road
Kwon Tong, Kowloon

Papercutz books maye be purchased for business or promtional use.
For information on bulk purchases please contact Macmillan Corporate and Premium
Sales Department at (800) 221-7945 x5442

Distributed by Macmillan
First Papercutz Printing

AH, THE LITTLE FAIRY GIRLS, THE LITTLE FAIRY GIRLS FROM HERE...

AH, THE LITTLE FAIRY GIRLS...

FOR A NICE BIRTHDAY PAR--*HIC!*-- PARTY. *HIC!*-- IT WAS NICE! *HIC!*

AH WELL, YOU DON'T TURN-- *HIC!*--450 YEARS OLD EVERY DAY!

OH, FAIRY GIRLS, OH, YOU FAIRY GIRLS, EVERYONE LOVES YOU! *HIC!*

?

WHAT'S THAT?

THAT LOOKED LIKE A... A...

A KOBOLD!

FOR ELF'S SAKE! IT'S A MEETING... WHY DID THEY ALL LEAVE THEIR CAVES?

MIDNIGHT ALREADY!

BONG BONG BONG BONG BONG BONG BONG

WHAT'S WRONG WITH IT? IT'S RINGING 13 TIMES!

BONG BONG BONG BONG BONG BONG BONG BONG

YOU COMING TO DRINK A PINT WITH US, PANDIGOLE?

?

WELL... UH... IT'S JUST...

HMM THAT'S NOT VERY DEFINITE!

SO, GOODNIGHT!

HEE HEE HEE!

SBONK

ELSEWHERE...

WHERE'S EARTH?

SHE WON'T BE LONG. WE HAVE A NEW MISSION!

NINA HAS MORE TREES TO OPEN?

YES, AND MORE THAN EVER, WE MUST BE...

...UNITED! AH HA HA!

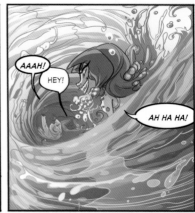

AAAH!

HEY!

AH HA HA!

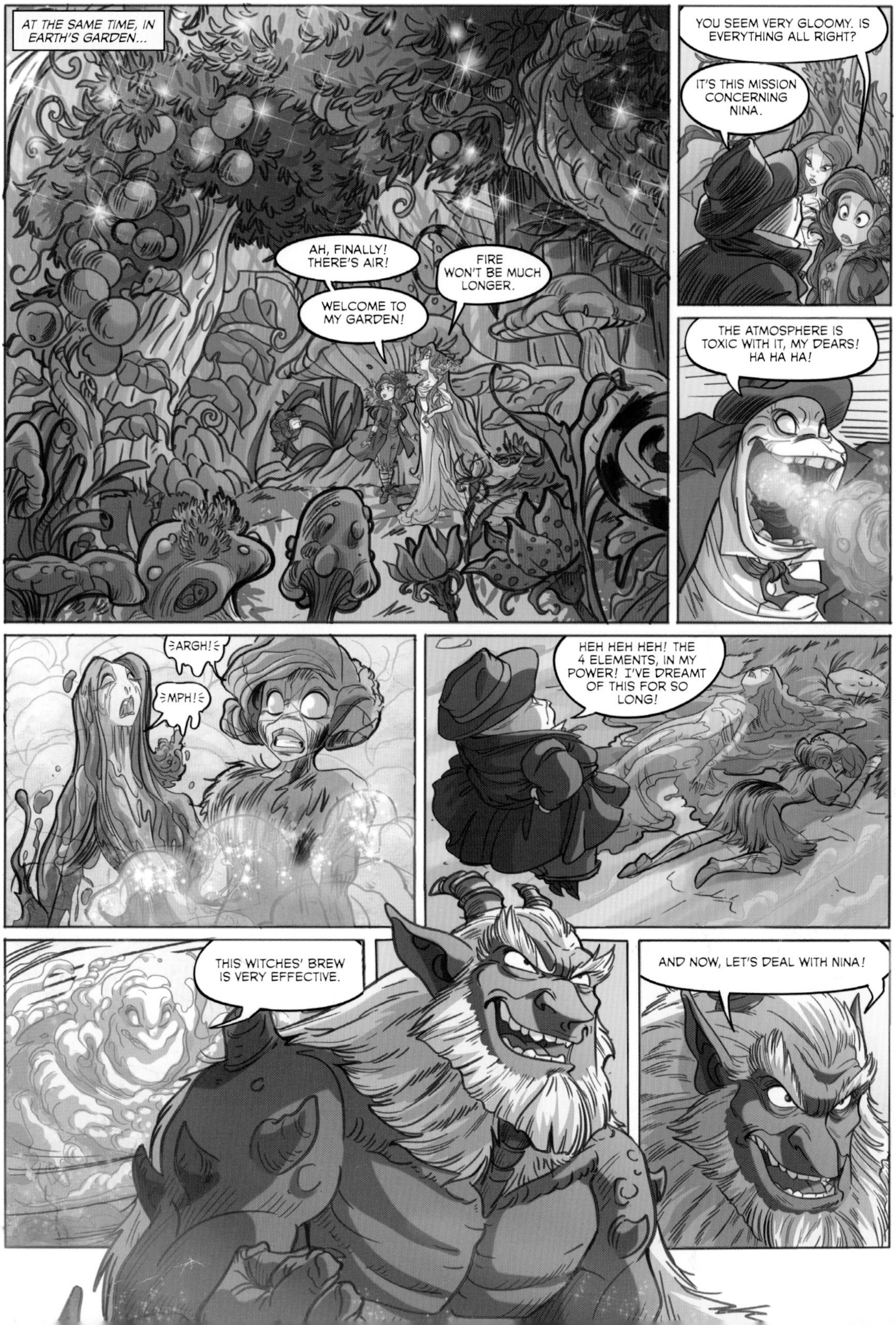
AT THE SAME TIME, IN EARTH'S GARDEN...
AH, FINALLY! THERE'S AIR!
WELCOME TO MY GARDEN!
FIRE WON'T BE MUCH LONGER.
YOU SEEM VERY GLOOMY. IS EVERYTHING ALL RIGHT?
IT'S THIS MISSION CONCERNING NINA.
THE ATMOSPHERE IS TOXIC WITH IT, MY DEARS! HA HA HA!
ARGH!
MPH!
HEH HEH HEH! THE 4 ELEMENTS, IN MY POWER! I'VE DREAMT OF THIS FOR SO LONG!
THIS WITCHES' BREW IS VERY EFFECTIVE.
AND NOW, LET'S DEAL WITH NINA!

THOSE NOISES... BY ANY CHANCE, COULD...

NINA IS SOUND ASLEEP.

I'M GETTING PARANOID. MY IMAGINATION'S PLAYING TRICKS ON ME!

THAT'S IMPOSSIBLE. NO ONE COULD BE OUT THERE...

WHAT DO WE DO? GO AHEAD?

NO! WE WAIT FOR ORDERS!

THE NEXT MORNING...

NOW'S THE TIME! LET'S GO!

KNOCK KNOCK

HMM?

WHAT COULD THAT BE? IT'S EARLY YET FOR THE MAIL.

QUIET, PRALINE!

WOOF, WOOF!

YES! WHAT IS IT...

?!

HELLO, MRS. IBBINS.

AAAAH!

HEE HEE! HEH HEH HEH!

ARRF!

WHAT DO WE DO NOW?

WE WAIT FOR THE BOSS!

AND THE MUTT?

ROLL THE OLD LADY UP IN A RUG.

AND WE CAN JUST EAT THE MUTT!

ARRF!

WOOF, WOOF, ARRF!

?

WHAT'S WRONG WITH THAT DOG NOW?

NOBODY'S EATING THAT DOG!

HELLO, MA'AM! SORRY FOR THE BOTHER. EXCUSE MY ASSISTANTS, THEY'RE *CLODS!* STAY CALM AND NOTHING WILL HAPPEN TO YOU.

NOW, GENTLEMEN, GET TO WORK! YOU HAVE NO ROOM FOR ERROR!

YES, GREAT MASTER!

AND NOW, THE HARD PART...

...GENTLY TELLING MY PARENTS

BUT IT'S A UNIQUE CHANCE, HONEY!

UH OH!

LIKE EVERY TIME!

YOU'VE BARELY BEEN BACK A MONTH, AFTER DISAPPEARING FOR A YEAR AND A HALF, AND YOU ALREADY WANT TO LEAVE AGAIN ON A RISKY ASSIGNMENT!

BUT IT'S AN *IMPORTANT* ASSIGNMENT!

OF COURSE, MORE IMPORTANT THAN YOUR *FAMILY!*

WHAT'S GOING ON?

YOUR FATHER'S *LEAVING* US ONCE AGAIN.

THAT'S NOT *FAIR,* ELSA. I'M JUST DOING MY JOB AS A *REPORTER!*

I GOT A TEXT FROM MY FRIEND ZACHARY IN THE WWF.*

THEY'RE HEADING OUT TOMORROW TO GO BLOCK JAPANESE WHALERS!

*WWF: WORLD WIDE FUND FOR NATURE

IT'S ONLY A *TWO-WEEK* TRIP.

OH? WELL, I WANTED TO TALK TO YOU BOTH ABOUT SOMETHING!

IT CAN WAIT TILL TONIGHT, NINA! WE'RE LATE AGAIN! ARE YOU READY?

BUT, MOM, IT'S REALLY IMPORTANT!

WE'LL TALK ABOUT IT TONIGHT!...

...IF YOUR FATHER WANTS TO LISTEN TO HIS FAMILY. HURRY UP AND GRAB YOUR BAG. WE'RE GOING!

QUICK, SYBIL! WE'RE RUNNING LATE, AND MOM'S IN A BAD MOOD!

MHMM-- WHAT? WHAT'S GOING ON?

BUT WHAT TIME IS IT?

WERE YOU STILL ASLEEP OR WHAT? HERE'S YOUR BREAKFAST! GET GOING!

HEY, CHILL OUT, NINA!

AND PANDIGOLE? HE'S STILL NOT HERE?

HE'S NOT IN THE BOTTOM OF THE BAG?

NO! HE'S BEEN GONE SINCE YESTERDAY EVENING! I'LL SET HIM STRAIGHT WHEN HE GETS BACK!

HE FELL ASLEEP AT THE PUB! HA HA HA!

NINA! HURRY UP! WE'RE GOING!

DO YOU THINK DADDY'S GOING TO LEAVE TO COVER THAT STORY?

I REALLY HOPE NOT!

UH, MOM?...

WHAT NOW?

I WANTED TO TALK TO YOU ABOUT SOMETHING.

GO ON, BE BRAVE! TELL HER!

I'D LIKE TO START *DANCE*.

WHAT?

BUT I THOUGHT YOU DIDN'T LIKE THAT!

ANYWAY, YOU TOOK *BOXING* AGAIN THIS YEAR! IT'S DECEMBER ALREADY, DO YOU KNOW HOW MUCH IT COSTS TO DO AN EXTRA ACTIVITY?

BUT, MOM! YOU WERE THE ONE WHO WANTED ME TO DO IT!

THE DISCUSSION IS CLOSED, NINA! WE'RE HERE. SEE YOU TONIGHT!

≶PFF!≶ YES, SEE YOU TONIGHT, MOM! GOODBYE, LEO!

COOL! ANTOINE'S HERE!

IN 275 YEARS OF SERVICE, IT'S THE FIRST TIME HE'S BEEN AWOL.

HEY, NINA! ARE YOU LISTENING TO ME? PANDIGOLE HAS DISAPPEARED, AND YOU DON'T GIVE A HOOT!

SYBIL, YOU HAVE TO HELP ME, IT'S TOO IMPORTANT!

I WANT TO DO *DANCE* INSTEAD OF *BOXING*!

YOU DON'T LIKE BOXING ANYMORE?

I DO! BUT A GIRL WHO *BOXES* SCARES AWAY BOYS! WHEREAS *DANCE*...

HE HE HE! AH YES, IT'S BECAUSE OF ANTOINE!

YOU WOULDN'T BE A LITTLE IN *LOVE*, WOULD YOU?

≶PFF!≶ *NO WAY!* YOU'RE REALLY AWFUL SOMETIMES.

BUT I HAVE TO BE A *SUPER* GREAT DANCER OR ELSE I'LL LOOK *RIDICULOUS!*

AND LAURIE'S IN THE DANCE CLASS, TOO, AND AMANITE WILL BE SURE TO GIVE YOU TROUBLE!

OKAY! FIRST CLASS THIS AFTERNOON! YOU'LL BE THE *SUPERSTAR* OF THE DANCE CLASS!

AWESOME! THAT'S COOL!

HELLO, EVERYONE!

BIG NEWS OF THE DAY: *I'M GOING TO DO DANCE!*

TA-*DAAAAA!*

YOU?

NO MORE *BOXING* THEN?

AND YOUR PARENTS *AGREE?*

THAT'S GREAT! DANCE IS A *LOT* COOLER THAN BOXING FOR A GIRL!

OH, YEAH, YOU THINK SO? MY PARENTS ARE REALLY HAPPY!

UHH, YOU WOULDN'T BE LYING A LITTLE THERE?

NO WAY! THEY'RE JUST NOT CONVINCED, THAT'S ALL!

WHO'S NOT CONVINCED, NINA?

UH... I... UMM...

YOU? DANCE? IT'LL BE "GOOSE LAKE" THEN?

HA HA HA!

≷PFF!≷ YOU'RE AWFUL, SONIA!

I THINK THAT'S GREAT! AND I'M SURE NINA WILL BE VERY TALENTED!

WHAT'S GOTTEN INTO LAURIE? SHE'S *DEFENDING* YOU NOW?

?

HEY, YEAH! MAYBE SHE'S TIRED OF ANNOYING ME ALL THE TIME!

WITH AMANITE FOR A BACKPACK FAIRY, I DON'T TRUST HER! SHE'S HIDING SOMETHING!

BAH, YOU SEE EVIL EVERY-WHERE!

GOOD JOB, LAURIE! KEEP SWEET-TALKING NINA LIKE THAT!

YES, IT'S *WORKING!* ANTOINE'S ALREADY PAYING ME A LITTLE MORE ATTENTION!

I'M TELLING YOU IT'S NOT NORMAL, NINA!...

AMANITE IS PLOTTING SOMETHING AGAINST YOU!

⋧PFF!⋦ YOU WEAR ME OUT WITH YOUR SUSPICIONS! YOU'RE COMPLETELY *PARANOID*, POOR SYBIL!

AH YES, *I'M* PARANOID! WELL, WE'LL SEE WHO'S RIGHT!

HOO! WHAT A TEMPER!

SO, NINA, READY FOR YOUR FIRST DANCE CLASS?

IT'S JUST... I DON'T HAVE AN OUTFIT. MY PARENTS AREN'T VERY ENTHUSED ABOUT ME CHANGING ACTIVITIES DURING THE YEAR.

NO PROBLEM! I HAVE *TONS* OF DANCE OUTFITS! I'LL GIVE YOU SOME!

GREAT! THANKS, LAURIE!

SEE YOU TOMORROW, TWINS!

I'LL GO WITH YOU, GIRLS!

IT IS PRETTY *WEIRD* FOR LAURIE TO BE SO NICE TO NINA!

⋧PFF!⋦ YOU GIRLS ARE ALWAYS IMAGINING THINGS!

12

THIS ENTRANCE FOR DANCERS ONLY! THAT WAY FOR VISITORS!

OKAY! SEE YOU SOON, GIRLS!

Dance School

HELLO, FIONA, LET ME INTRODUCE A NEW GIRL, NINA!

HELLO! WELCOME, NINA!

WHAT THE HECK HAVE I GOTTEN MYSELF INTO? ALL THIS TO PLEASE ANTOINE! I'LL BE *AWFUL!*

LET ME HANDLE IT, AND YOU WON'T BE RIDICULOUS!

I WANT TO FORGET ABOUT IT! EVERYBODY WILL LAUGH!

HERE, NINA! IT'S THE LATEST STYLE!

YOU'LL BE GREAT! I'LL MEET YOU IN THE STUDIO!

SO MUCH KINDNESS FROM HER REALLY ISN'T *NORMAL.* I WONDER WHAT SHE'S COOKING UP?

SHE'S SIMPLY BECOME NICE, THAT'S ALL.

YOU'RE FORGETTING ALL THE DIRTY TRICKS SHE'S PULLED ON YOU!

AND EVERYTHING SHE'S TRIED TO DO AGAINST YOU WITH AMANITE, HER BACKPACK FAIRY.

NO, I HAVEN'T FORGOTTEN!

BUT EVERYONE CAN MAKE A MISTAKE AND GET A SECOND CHANCE!

BEFORE WE START, LET'S WELCOME NINA TO OUR CLASS.

NINA, YOU'LL SHOW US WHAT YOU KNOW HOW TO DO AS A LITTLE EVALUATION!

AY YI YI!

LET YOUR BODY MOVE AND LET YOUR FEET DO THEIR THING!

NOVEAT ANIMATES GOSSIPTUM!

WOW! SHE'S AWESOME!

OOPS! SORRY.

BRAVO, NINA! NOT BAD, NOT BAD AT ALL!

HEE HEE! THE DANCE SPELL ALWAYS HAS A GREAT EFFECT!

WHAT?!

SURPRISE!

SLAM

AMANITE, NO! NO!

OKAY, LADIES! THAT'LL BE ALL FOR TONIGHT!

TILL NEXT WEEK!

NICE NUMBER, NINA! GOOD JOB!

THANKS, LAURIE!

AND THANKS, SYBIL! TOO BAD ONLY I CAN HEAR HER AND SEE HER...

...BECAUSE SHE COULD CONVINCE MOM!

14

ACTUALLY, *DON'T* THANK SYBIL! THAT'S PART OF THE RULES OF LIVING WITH A BACKPACK FAIRY!*

*HURRY! SEE THE PREVIOUS VOLUMES!

WHERE'D SHE GO, THOUGH?

MY PHONE. A NEW MESSAGE.

OH, IT'S MOM!

Dad has left on assignment. Neighbor's watching Leo. I have a meeting tonight. Counting on you to get home soon, honey. Kisses and hugs.

SO, DAD LEFT ANYWAY...

AND HERE WE ARE, ALL THREE OF US, WITHOUT HIM ONCE AGAIN!

NINA, HURRY UP AND CHANGE! THE SCHOOL IS CLOSING! AND KEEP THE OUTFIT, I HAVE OTHERS AT HOME.

UH--THANKS, LAURIE. YOU'RE TOO KIND!

A BIT LATER...

THAT WAS *GREAT*, NINA!

YOU REALLY DANCE LIKE A PRO!

UH--YES, YES!

AH, MY PARENTS' DRIVER IS WAITING FOR ME! I'LL SEE YOU!

LAURIE, I WANTED TO TELL YOU, I THINK IT'S REALLY NICE WHAT YOU DID FOR NINA!

AWW, IT'S NOTHING, BABE! YOU'RE SO SWEET! CIAO, LOVEBIRDS!

LAURIE'S REALLY *NICE!* NOT AT ALL LIKE THE TWINS DESCRIBED HER!

YES, SHE'S REALLY *CHANGED!*

YOU LOOK ANNOYED! IS SOMETHING WRONG?

NO, NO! IT'S OKAY! I JUST HAVE TO GET HOME QUICK. THE NEIGHBOR IS WATCHING MY BROTHER, AND I DON'T WANT TO LEAVE HIM WITH THAT OLD BIDDY! SHE'S ALWAYS SPYING ON EVERYONE AND GOSSIPING!

AND SYBIL? WHERE HAS SHE DISAPPEARED TO?

WINDOW-SHOPPING AGAIN, SURELY! THE POOR FASHION VICTIM!

OOF --- AMANITE! THAT PEST!

HEY! MAGICAL BONDS!

SO, DID YOU SLEEP WELL, CUTIE?

WELCOME, MY PRETTY!

KOBOLDS, YOU DIRTY LITTLE RATS! WHAT HAVE YOU DONE TO PANDIGOLE?

OH, NOTHING AT ALL! A LITTLE BOP ON THE HEAD AND A FEW PINTS OF BEER!

THE RESULT: THE GENTLEMAN'S SLEEPING LIKE A LOG!

KOBOLDS ARE MORE STUPID THAN MEAN. IF I COULD CONVINCE THEM...

SET US FREE, BECAUSE IF OBERON, OUR KING, FINDS OUT, YOU'LL BE RISKING HIS WRATH!

UH...

HEY, GUYS! HERE'S A THIRD PACKAGE TO KEEP WARM!

PUT IT HERE! WE'LL PAMPER IT LIKE THE TWO OTHERS! HEE HEE HEE!

MRS. IBBINS, NINA'S NEIGHBOR! BUT THEN...

BY THE SPIRIT OF THE FAIRIES, NINA IS IN *GRAVE DANGER!*

SYBIL AND DAD HAVE GONE I DON'T KNOW WHERE, BUT I FEEL REALLY GOOD TONIGHT! I'M HAPPY!

NINA?... NINA! ARE YOU DAYDREAMING? WE'RE AT YOUR PLACE.

AH YES! THANKS FOR THE WALK, ANTOINE. SEE YOU TOMORROW!

SEE YOU TOMORROW, NINA! QUICK, GO FREE YOUR BROTHER FROM THE WITCH! HA HA HA!

SMACK

YES, I'LL HURRY AND DO THAT! IT'S TRUE THAT SHE'S LIKE A WITCH! HEE HEE HEE!

OOPS! GOOD EVENING, MRS. IBBINS!

HELLO, NINA! WHAT WITCH ARE YOU TALKING ABOUT?

WOOF WOOF!

UH-- HEH HEH! OUR MATH TEACHER!

THANKS FOR WATCHING LEO, MRS. IBBINS!

WHERE'S OUR CAT, MACAROON?

I PUT HIM OUTSIDE! MY LULU CAN'T STAND CATS!

WOOF! YIP YIP YIP!

OKAY, I'LL TAKE OVER FROM HERE! THANKS AGAIN, MRS. IBBINS!

IS LEO IN HIS BEDROOM?

YES, IN HIS BED. HE MUST BE SLEEPING FOR NOW.

I'LL GO SEE HIM.

YOU HAVE PLENTY OF TIME, NINA. TELL ME A LITTLE ABOUT YOUR DAY.

MY DAY? WHY WOULD YOU--

GROOO!

LEO?

LEO!

GROOO!

STAY HERE, NINA!

WHAT'S GOING ON UP THERE?

MY GOD, LEO!

GRAOOO!

NINA! STAY HERE, YOU LITTLE PEST!

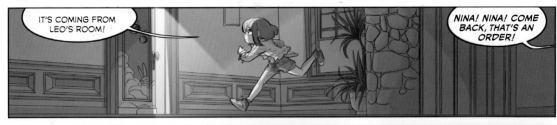

IT'S COMING FROM LEO'S ROOM!

NINA! NINA! COME BACK, THAT'S AN ORDER!

LEO! ARE YOU OKAY?

?!

A DRAGON?!

LEO-- IT--IT ATE LEO!

GIVE ME BACK MY BROTHER, YOU FILTHY BEAST! LET GO OF HIS TEDDY BEAR!

GROOO!

GO AWAY! GIVE LEO BACK TO ME!

≡GROWL!≡

?

18

=ROAR!=

CRAASH

OH, NO!

STOP! STAY HERE!

=GROWL!=

CRASH

?

NINA!

BE CALM, DRAGON! NICE DRAGON!

SYBIL WILL COME! SHE'LL FIX EVERYTHING!

GROOMPF!

GROOO!

NOOOO! DON'T LEAVE!

GROOO!

STAY HERE!

NINA! WHAT *WAS* THAT THING?!

19

MY HANDS! THEY'RE SLIPPING!

NO, I CAN'T LOSE MY GRIP!

NO! I'M GOING TO FALL OFF!

NOOOO!

AAAAAH!

I'M GOING TO CRASH IN THE PARK!

NINA!

AAAH! WHAT'S--

PLOP

AAAH! LEMME GO, YOU BIG MONSTER!

NICE WELCOME FOR A FRIEND!

PUCK?!

HELLO, CUTIE!

PUCK! WHAT ARE YOU DOING HERE?!

LIKE MANY SPIRITS OF THE FOREST, I CAN TRANSFORM WITH EASE! THAT'S USEFUL WHEN SOMEONE'S FALLING FROM THE SKY!

BUT LISTEN CLOSELY. I HAVE LITTLE TIME!

YOU HAVE A NEW TREE TO OPEN, ON OBERON'S ORDERS. DO IT QUICKLY, NINA!

WHAT ABOUT SYBIL? AND THE DRAGON?

THAT BABY IS HARDLY A DRAGON! BEWARE OF LACK--?

NINA! NINA! ARE YOU THERE?

WHAT THE DEVIL-- A HUMAN! NO MORTAL BUT YOU MUST SEE ME!

IT'S ANTOINE! BUT--WAIT, PUCK!

NIN-- OUCH!

OH, ANTOINE! IT-- I-- I--

ARE YOU OKAY? ARE YOU HURT? WHAT HAPPENED HERE?

IT'S LEO! AND SYBIL STILL ISN'T HERE!

LEO? YOUR BROTHER? AND WHO'S SYBIL?

I'M OKAY, I'M OKAY, ANTOINE! I'M SORRY BUT...

...I CAN'T TELL YOU.

WHAT CAN'T YOU TELL ME?

NOTHING. I'M BEGGING YOU, DON'T INSIST! YOU WOULDN'T UNDERSTAND!

YOU DON'T TRUST ME? IS THAT IT?

PLEASE, THINGS ARE ALREADY SO COMPLICATED...

I HAVE TO GO HOME. MY MOM'S COMING. TRUST ME, ANTOINE!

HOW? YOU HIDE THINGS FROM ME AND YOU WANT ME TO ACT LIKE NOTHING HAPPENED?

YOU CAN'T ORDER ME AROUND, NINA! IF WE LIE TO EACH OTHER, NOTHING WILL WORK!

I THOUGHT WE TRUSTED EACH OTHER! LAURIE, AT LEAST, DOESN'T SPOUT NONSENSE AT ME!

I WAS NAÏVE! GOODNIGHT, NINA. HAVE FUN WITH YOUR NEW FRIENDS!

ANTOINE...

ANTOINE...

WHY AM I SO ALONE?

SYBIL, HELP!

AND HERE'S SOME BIG NEWS, MY DEAR LAURIE!

AMANITE, MY DEAR BACKPACK FAIRY, IT'D BEST BE EXCELLENT NEWS!

IT IS! ANTOINE AND NINA HAVE ARGUED, AND SYBIL'S OUT OF ACTION!

ARE YOU SURE? IT'S TOO GOOD TO BE TRUE!

SEE FOR YOUR-SELF!

OOOH! POOR, POOR NINA!

ANGRY WITH EACH OTHER AT THE START OF SUCH A PRETTY LOVE STORY. IT'S SO SAD!

AND HER BACKPACK FAIRY?

LET'S SAY SHE'S TEMPORARILY UNABLE TO HELP NINA! HEE HEE HEE!

HEE HEE HEE! GREAT! YOU'RE SO AWESOME, AMANITE!

I ABSOLUTELY MUST GET FREE. ∋HMMPF!∈ THESE MAGICAL BONDS ARE IMPOSSIBLE TO BREAK!

THE KOBOLDS ARE TOO STUPID TO HAVE DEVISED THESE ABDUCTIONS ON THEIR OWN!

ONE THING'S CERTAIN, THIS WHOLE PLOT IS TARGETING NINA.

IF ONLY PANDIGOLE WOULD WAKE UP!

PANDIGOLE! *PANDIGOLE!*

HMM...? UGN?...WHO'S CALLING ME?

AH, BRAVO! 275 YEARS OF GOOD AND FAITHFUL SERVICE TO END UP ACTING LIKE THE FIRST TROLL WHO COMES ALONG!

OWW! YES, BUT DON'T SHOUT! MY HEAD'S BEATING LIKE A DRUM!

HEY, THOSE IDIOT KOBOLDS FORGOT TO TIE ME UP!

HEE HEE HEE!

OR THEY FIGURED YOU WERE TOO STUPID TO BE DANGEROUS.

YEAH, OKAY! HOW DO WE GET OUT OF HERE NOW?

LISTEN CLOSELY TO ME.

THERE'S A SPELL TO DISSOLVE MAGICAL BONDS--

BUT IT ONLY WORKS IF IT'S SAID BY SOMEONE WHO'S FREE.

REPEAT AFTER ME: "MUSILA GARROTIS LINICI!"

UH... "MUSILA CARROTES, LYCHEE!"

UH, NO, NO! "MUSILA GARROTLI NINISSI!"

YOU'D BETTER SAY THAT SPELL CORRECTLY AND FAST BEFORE I CHANGE YOU INTO A HAIRY TURNIP!

YES, YES, SYBIL! I'M CONCENTRATING!

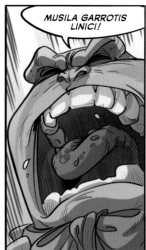

MUSILA GARROTIS LINICI!

ZWOOUFF

AWESOME! IT WORKED!

THE NEIGHBOR'S STILL IN A DAZE.

WE'LL LEAVE HER HERE. SHE'S IN NO DANGER.

NOBODY IN SIGHT! THE KOBOLDS HAVE DISAPPEARED!

THOSE CREATURES ARE TOO ERRATIC. THEY HAVE NO FOCUS AT ALL.

WHOEVER MADE USE OF THEIR SERVICES DIDN'T GET A GOOD DEAL.

EVERYTHING SEEMS QUIET IN THE HOUSE.

MRS. IBBINS HAS LEFT, EVIDENTLY.

BUT SHE WAS ACTING REALLY WEIRD.

NINA!

AAAHH!

SYBIL! PANDIGOLE!

YOU'RE FINALLY HERE!

WE'RE ALONE. MANY THINGS HAVE HAPPENED SINCE YOU DISAPPEARED!

I WAS KIDNAPPED BY KOBOLDS, JUST LIKE PANDIGOLE!

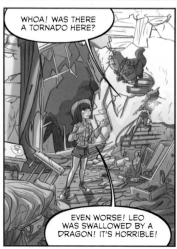

WHOA! WAS THERE A TORNADO HERE?

EVEN WORSE! LEO WAS SWALLOWED BY A DRAGON! IT'S HORRIBLE!

25

A FEW EXPLANATIONS LATER...

AND MOM'S GOING TO ARRIVE ANY MOMENT NOW! WHAT CAN WE *DO*, SYBIL?

HERE YOU GO! MR. MAN IS GONE AGAIN AND I'M STUCK WITH THE KIDS AND MY JOB TO HANDLE, NOT INCLUDING EVERYTHING ELSE!

HEY! LOOK OUT!

SQUEEEE

BANG

?

?

MOMMY!

APPARENTLY THE NOISE DIDN'T AWAKE ANYONE!

MOM! ARE YOU OKAY?

OH, NINA... YES, YES, I'M ALL RIGHT. JUST A LITTLE DAZED!

LEAN ON ME! THE HOUSE IS RIGHT HERE!

NOBODY IN SIGHT! I CAN DO A LITTLE MAGIC!

CORRICOLO BRISKA TILBURY OMNIBUS!

YOU REST, MOM! IT'S ALL RIGHT.

LUCKILY SYBIL IS HERE!

NOW HOW DO I EXPLAIN TO HER ABOUT LEO?

AND HUP! ONE REPAIRED CAR!

WHERE'S YOUR BROTHER? WHERE'S LEO?

UH, LEO? HE'S SLEEPING, MOM!

OKAY. I'LL PULL MYSELF TO-GETHER AND GO GIVE HIM A KISS.

I CAN'T BELIEVE IT! I NEARLY RAN OVER A CHILD!

⸫PFFF⸫ AND THAT LAZY PANDIGOLE WENT TO GO SLEEP!

NINA! YOUR MOTHER MUSTN'T BUDGE FROM HERE SO LONG AS WE HAVEN'T FOUND LEO!

I KNOW, BUT HOW CAN WE STOP HER?

I'LL PUT HER INTO A SLEEP TILL WE FIX EVERYTHING. TRUST ME.

WHAT? ARE YOU *CRAZY?* AND WHAT IF SOMETHING HAPPENED TO HER, TOO?

NO, DON'T WORRY! IT'LL BE LIKE WITH LEONARDO DA VINCI!* TRUST ME!

TRUST? I DON'T KNOW WHOM TO TRUST RIGHT NOW!

* SEE SYBIL #4 "PRINCESS NINA."

TRUST IN THE TWO OF US! WE'VE ALWAYS SUCCEEDED TOGETHER!

SOMMULAE PASSIFLORE JOUANI-GOTE!

MHMM...

OKAY! TO RECAP: THE KOBOLDS AND AMANITE ARE UP TO SOME-THING, MRS. IBBINS WAS ABDUCTED FOR SOME-ONE TO TAKE HER PLACE...

...AND THAT A DRAGON SWALLOWED LEO, AND PUCK CAME TO TALK TO ME ABOUT A TREE.

27

AND TO MAKE IT WORSE, THE DRAGON *DEMOLISHED* LEO'S BEDROOM AFTER *SWALLOWING* HIM!

THAT'S CURIOUS, TOO!

WHAT'S CURIOUS?

HMMM... WELL...

IT HAD TO HAVE BEEN A YOUNG, INEXPERIENCED DRAGON. AN ADULT DRAGON WOULD HAVE BURNED EVERYTHING.

WHAT DO YOU MEAN?

I MEAN WE STILL HAVE A CHANCE TO SAVE LEO!

BUT FIRST, WE HAVE TO REPAIR EVERYTHING THE DRAGON BROKE! *AVENTUM BRISUS EPARIS!*

SO, LET'S GO SEARCH FOR LEO! EVEN IF I HAVE TO GUT THAT DRAGON MYSELF!

WE MUST FIND PUCK AGAIN! HE'LL KNOW WHERE WE SHOULD SEARCH!

AND MOM? WE CAN'T LEAVE HER ALONE LIKE THIS! WHAT IF THE KOBOLDS COME BACK WITH THE *FAKE* MRS. IBBINS?

WELL, THEY'LL GET THEMSELVES GOBBLED UP BY *MR. MACAROON!*

CATSOMANIS PANTAGRUELUS!

AND NOW, I DECLARE IT TO BE DRAGON HUNTING SEASON!

TALLYHO!

A SHORT TRIP LATER...

WHOA! THESE WHIRLWINDS ARE REALLY *FAST!*

AH! SYBIL!! ≥HUFF≥ ≥PUFF≥ FINALLY!

AH, PUCK! YOU'RE HERE!

I WAS WAITING FOR YOU. I COULDN'T GO BACK DOWN AMONG THE HUMANS!

VERY SERIOUS THINGS ARE HAPPENING! WE MUST BE DISCREET!

OBERON, OUR KING, DOESN'T KNOW ANY-THING YET!

EVEN THE FOUR ELEMENTS HAVE DISAP-PEARED!

AH, MY KEYS!

I'LL HAVE TO SORT THEM ONE OF THESE DAYS. SOME OF THEM DON'T HAVE A LOCK ANYMORE!

THIS IS THE TREASURE ROOM. YOU'RE THE FIRST HUMAN TO ENTER HERE. BUT HERE'S WHAT'S MOST TERRIBLE--

WOW! IT'S SO *BEAUTIFUL!*

THE MAP OF TREES WAS STOLEN TWO DAYS AGO!

THE THIEVES CAME THROUGH THIS HOLE!

A TUNNEL, GALLERIES WITH SUPPORTS-- A PROFESSIONAL JOB! IT STINKS OF THE KOBOLDS!

SHHHHH! QUIET DOWN! IF THE KING LEARNS OF THIS, WE'RE ALL DOOMED!

WELL, IF THEY MANAGED TO COME HERE THROUGH THIS TUNNEL, WE SHOULD BE ABLE TO FIND THEM AT THE OTHER END!

BE CAREFUL. THE TUNNEL COULD CLOSE UP AT ANY MOMENT!

29

WHAT DID HE MEAN BY "CLOSE UP"?

A KOBOLD TUNNEL CAN ONLY BE USED BY KOBOLDS.

AND SINCE WE'RE NOT KOBOLDS...

...THE TUNNEL COULD *COLLAPSE!*

NICE-- VERY REASSURING!

THAT DIDN'T TAKE LONG!

RUMBLE RUMBLE

RUN, NINA, RUN!

LET'S TAKE THAT MINING CAR!

OVER THERE! A LIGHT!

RUMBLE BOOM

OH, NO! NOW I HAVE TO THROW AWAY MY BEAUTIFUL OUTFIT!

SYBIL, *LOOK!*

ONE OF THE *TREES* TO BE OPENED!

LET'S NOT WASTE ANY TIME THEN!

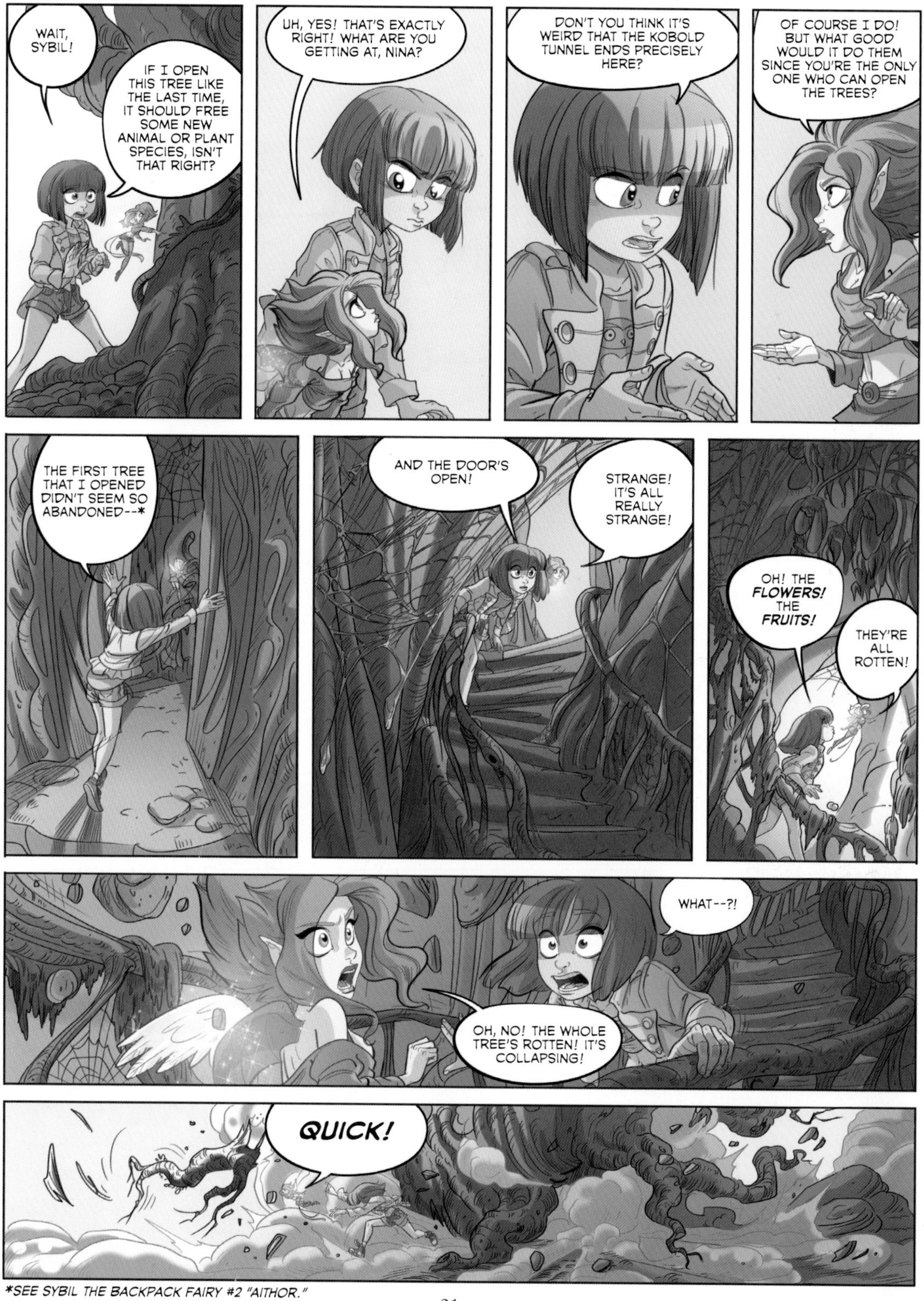
WAIT, SYBIL!
IF I OPEN THIS TREE LIKE THE LAST TIME, IT SHOULD FREE SOME NEW ANIMAL OR PLANT SPECIES, ISN'T THAT RIGHT?
UH, YES! THAT'S EXACTLY RIGHT! WHAT ARE YOU GETTING AT, NINA?
DON'T YOU THINK IT'S WEIRD THAT THE KOBOLD TUNNEL ENDS PRECISELY HERE?
OF COURSE I DO! BUT WHAT GOOD WOULD IT DO THEM SINCE YOU'RE THE ONLY ONE WHO CAN OPEN THE TREES?
THE FIRST TREE THAT I OPENED DIDN'T SEEM SO ABANDONED--*
AND THE DOOR'S OPEN!
STRANGE! IT'S ALL REALLY STRANGE!
OH! THE **FLOWERS!** THE **FRUITS!**
THEY'RE ALL ROTTEN!
WHAT--?!
OH, NO! THE WHOLE TREE'S ROTTEN! IT'S COLLAPSING!
QUICK!

*SEE SYBIL THE BACKPACK FAIRY #2 "AITHOR."

I DON'T UNDERSTAND ANYTHING NOW! EVERYTHING'S COLLAPSING AROUND US! ALL THE PATHS ARE DISAPPEARING ONE AFTER THE OTHER!

EVERYTHING'S DEAD HERE! HOW WILL WE GET BACK?

MAYBE I COULD DO SOMETHING ABOUT THAT.

PUCK!

YES! I DIDN'T HAVE THE HEART TO LEAVE YOU ALONE, LITTLE LADIES! I FOLLOWED YOU INTO THE TUNNEL!

GREAT! SO LET'S QUESTION THAT LITTLE STINK BUG AMANITE! LET'S GET GOING!

BUT HOW? THE TUNNEL IS BLOCKED, AND YOU CAN'T CREATE A WHIRLWIND IN THIS DESERT!

DO YOU HAVE DOUBTS ABOUT MY SHAPE-CHANGING ABILITIES?

AND PRESTO! A LITTLE TRANSFOR-MATION!

IF THE YOUNG LADIES WOULD BE SO KIND AS TO CLIMB ABOARD.

THERE'S SOMETHING ELSE THAT YOU DON'T KNOW.

IF IT'S MORE BAD NEWS, YOU CAN KEEP IT!

THE FOUR ELEMENTS STILL HAVEN'T REAPPEARED!

FROM HERE ON OUT, WE'RE THE ONLY ONES WHO CAN TAKE ACTION!

WE ABSOLUTELY HAVE TO MAKE AMANITE TALK!

HOW WILL YOU MAKE AMANITE COME OUT? SHE MUST BE ON GUARD AND WE CAN'T WAKE THE WHOLE NEIGHBORHOOD!

IT DOESN'T MATTER. AMANITE ISN'T HERE. I DON'T FEEL HER PRESENCE!

HMM...

WHAT WILL WE DO THEN?

SYBIL'S RIGHT. STAYING HERE IS USELESS! LET'S GO BACK TO THE HOUSE. WE ABSOLUTELY MUST FIND ANOTHER SOLUTION BEFORE DAWN!

AND FIND MY SWEET, LITTLE LEO AGAIN!

OH! LOOK! AT MRS. IBBINS'!

KOBOLDS! THEY'VE COME BACK!

LET'S LAY LOW!

WHY ARE WE BRINGING BACK THE OLD LADY AND HER DOG?

WE DON'T NEED HER ANYMORE. THE MASTER GOT WHAT HE WANTED AT THE GIRL'S HOUSE!

I'D HAVE LIKED TO HAVE EATEN THE DOG!

AND WHAT IF SHE TALKS AFTER WAKING UP?

THERE'S NO DANGER! WITH THE MASTER'S POTION, SHE'LL HAVE FORGOTTEN EVERYTHING!

WHO ARE THEY TALKING ABOUT?

WE'LL FIND OUT VERY SOON.

?

HEY! ⇒PSST!⇐

GOOD NIGHT! HEE HEE HEE!

BONK

OW!

YES!

BUT--

WHAT ARE YOU PLANNING TO DO WITH THE KOBOLD?

THE TACTIC OF THE TROJAN HORSE IS STILL EFFECTIVE!

THIS SHAPE-SHIFTING GIFT IS USEFUL!

LATER, GIRLS! TRY TO FIND OUT MORE FROM THAT FELLOW!

PUCK, WAIT!

≥GRRR!≤ HOW WILL WE FIND HIM AGAIN? HE'S WALKING INTO THE LION'S DEN!

LET'S INTERROGATE THE GOBLIN!

MMM...

WHERE'S YOUR HIDEOUT? WHAT ARE YOU PLOTTING?

WHERE'S LEO, MY LITTLE BROTHER?

TALK, OR I'LL TELL MY FAT CAT TO DEVOUR YOU!

≥GULP!≤

NO, NO! KEEP HOLD OF YOUR MONSTER! I'LL TALK!

I DON'T KNOW WHERE WE'RE TO MEET! ALL I KNOW IS THAT IT'S REALLY HOT THERE!

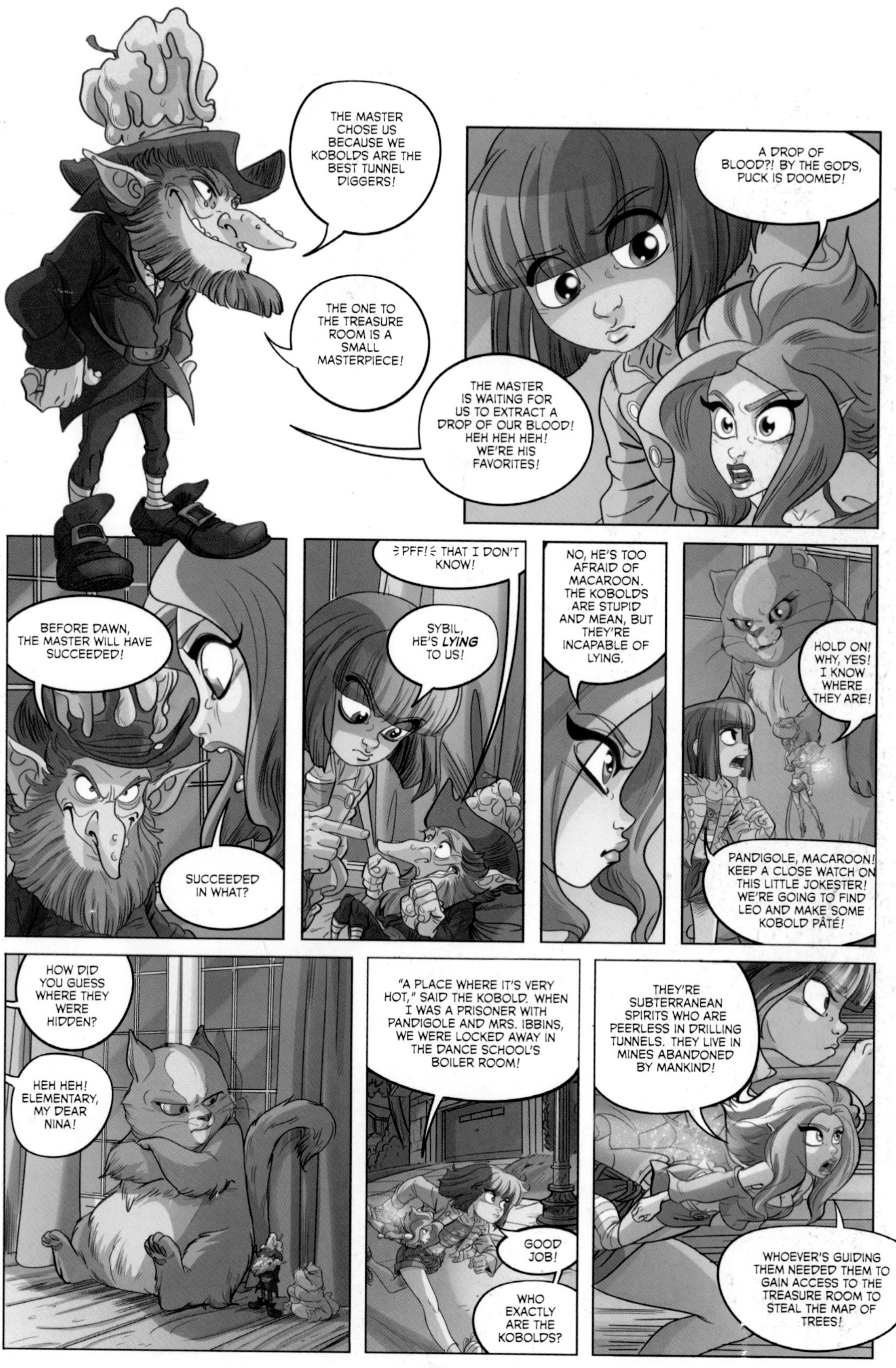
THE MASTER CHOSE US BECAUSE WE KOBOLDS ARE THE BEST TUNNEL DIGGERS!
THE ONE TO THE TREASURE ROOM IS A SMALL MASTERPIECE!
THE MASTER IS WAITING FOR US TO EXTRACT A DROP OF OUR BLOOD! HEH HEH HEH! WE'RE HIS FAVORITES!
A DROP OF BLOOD?! BY THE GODS, PUCK IS DOOMED!
BEFORE DAWN, THE MASTER WILL HAVE SUCCEEDED!
SUCCEEDED IN WHAT?
PFF! THAT I DON'T KNOW!
SYBIL, HE'S ***LYING*** TO US!
NO, HE'S TOO AFRAID OF MACAROON. THE KOBOLDS ARE STUPID AND MEAN, BUT THEY'RE INCAPABLE OF LYING.
HOLD ON! WHY, YES! I KNOW WHERE THEY ARE!
PANDIGOLE, MACAROON! KEEP A CLOSE WATCH ON THIS LITTLE JOKESTER! WE'RE GOING TO FIND LEO AND MAKE SOME KOBOLD PÂTÉ!
HOW DID YOU GUESS WHERE THEY WERE HIDDEN?
HEH HEH! ELEMENTARY, MY DEAR NINA!
"A PLACE WHERE IT'S VERY HOT," SAID THE KOBOLD. WHEN I WAS A PRISONER WITH PANDIGOLE AND MRS. IBBINS, WE WERE LOCKED AWAY IN THE DANCE SCHOOL'S BOILER ROOM!
GOOD JOB!
WHO EXACTLY ARE THE KOBOLDS?
THEY'RE SUBTERRANEAN SPIRITS WHO ARE PEERLESS IN DRILLING TUNNELS. THEY LIVE IN MINES ABANDONED BY MANKIND!
WHOEVER'S GUIDING THEM NEEDED THEM TO GAIN ACCESS TO THE TREASURE ROOM TO STEAL THE MAP OF TREES!

WHY DID YOU SAY THAT PUCK WAS DOOMED?

THE MASTER WANTS A DROP OF BLOOD FROM EACH KOBOLD. THEY HAVE BROWN BLOOD...

...BUT PUCK'S IS GREEN!

HOW DO YOU KNOW IT'S HERE? THERE ARE LOTS OF OTHER BOILER ROOMS IN THE CITY!

IT'S THE BIGGEST ONE! IT ALSO SERVES THE TOWN HALL AND THE ELEMENTARY SCHOOL.

IT'S ALL LOCKED UP! WE CAN'T GET IN!

YOU CAN BE SO FOOLISH SOMETIMES!

PICOLETIS PALASTRUS ELOQUUS!

LADIES FIRST, IF YOU PLEASE...

WATCH OUT FOR A POSSIBLE WELCOMING COMMITTEE!

LOOK OUT! SOMEONE'S COMING!

LET'S HURRY. THE INCUBATION OF THE EGGS WILL SOON BE OVER.

YES, THE MASTER WAS ALREADY FURIOUS THAT WE LET THE FAIRY AND HER PANDIGOLE GET AWAY.

WE SHOULD HAVE TIED HIM UP!

QUICK! QUICK! THE MASTER NEEDS US!

WE'RE ON THE RIGHT TRACK!

LET'S FOLLOW THEM QUIETLY!

COME IN, COME IN, MY FRIENDS!

WE'RE HERE!

COME SEE WHO CAME TO SPY ON OUR LITTLE UNDERTAKING!

BY THE SPIRITS, PUCK HAS BEEN REVEALED!

TIE UP OUR FRIEND! HE'LL BE ABLE TO ADMIRE THE AWESOME SCIENCE OF THE GREAT LACKORS!

YES, GREAT MASTER!

LACKORS!

ONE OF THE MOST POWERFUL SORCERERS OF THE CURSED WORLD!

THE BIG, UGLY ONE OVER THERE?

BESIDE HIM IS THE DRAGON THAT SWALLOWED LEO!

AND IN THE GLASS JARS, THE FOUR ELEMENTS!

HE HAS THEM, TOO!

I DON'T SEE AMANITE. I DON'T SENSE HER EITHER!

BECAUSE YOU THINK THERE AREN'T ENOUGH DANGEROUS CREATURES HERE?

MY FRIENDS, THANKS TO YOU, I'M NEARING MY GOAL! MY FINAL, GRAND WORK!

HERE, A FEW DROPS OF YOUR BLOOD MIXED WITH A CELL FROM EACH OF THE FOUR ELEMENTS...

...TO WHICH I'VE ADDED THE SAP OF ONE OF THOSE FAMOUS TREES OF SPECIES!

HERE'S A POTION THAT'LL SPREAD OVER THESE MAGNIFICENT DRAGON EGGS...

...WHICH WILL GIVE BIRTH TO MARVELOUS, LITTLE DRAGONS WHOSE FOUL BREATH WILL EXTINGUISH ALL PLANT AND ANIMAL LIFE ON THIS EARTH!

WITH THESE DEAR LITTLE ONES WILL I BE BEGIN MY REIGN! HA HA HA!

BY DOING THAT, YOU'RE CONDEMNING THE WHOLE FAIRY WORLD TO DEATH!

THAT'S HORRENDOUS! WHAT CAN WE DO?

LET ME THINK!

THE COCKTAIL IS LACKING ONLY A FEW DROPS OF BLOOD FROM THIS YOUNG DRAGON!

RELAX, LITTLE ONE, YOU WON'T FEEL A THING!

YEEEE!

SY-- SYBIL... THE-- THE DRAGON!

IT'S-- IT'S TRANSFORMING!

FWOOF

LEO?!

DID YOU KNOW THAT?!

LET'S JUST SAY I SUSPECTED!

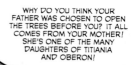

WHY DO YOU THINK YOUR FATHER WAS CHOSEN TO OPEN THE TREES BEFORE YOU? IT ALL COMES FROM YOUR MOTHER! SHE'S ONE OF THE MANY DAUGHTERS OF TITANIA AND OBERON!

≶BWAAAAHH!≶

SILENCE, WORM! DON'T DISTURB MY CONCENTRA- TION!

AND STOP FIDDLING WITH THAT FILTHY RAG!

TEDDY! TEDDY! ≶BWAA!≶

LEAVE MY BROTHER ALONE, YOU BIG LARVA!

NINA!

WELL, WELL! YOU'RE NOT A VERY POLITE FAMILY!

YOU WILL MAKE A NICE FIRST BREAKFAST FOR MY FUTURE, BABY DRAGONS!

LET HER GO, LACKORS! OR I'LL SHOW YOU!

CALM DOWN, FASHION VICTIM! YOU'LL CREASE YOUR PRETTY LITTLE OUTFIT AGAIN!

OUCH!

THIS WAY, LITTLE FAIRY! HEE HEE HEE!

SYBIL!

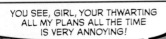

YOU SEE, GIRL, YOUR THWARTING ALL MY PLANS ALL THE TIME IS VERY ANNOYING!

I WANTED TO NEUTRALIZE YOU WHILE ALSO KIDNAPPING YOUR YOUNG DRAGON-BROTHER.

BUT YOU JUST HAD TO HANG ON TO HIM AND ESCAPE ME! BUT NOW I HAVE YOU, MY PRETTY, AND MY LITTLE PROTÉGÉS WILL ENJOY...

...SAVORING YOU ALL BOILED WHEN THEY HATCH FROM THEIR EGGS!

NOOOO! HELP!

NINA!

GROOAWW

?!

GROOAWW

ROAAAAR

AAAH! FILTHY BEAST!

HEY!

OUCH! CLOSE CALL!

⸴AAARH!⸵ YOU'LL PAY FOR THAT, YOU FILTHY BRAT!

WHOOOOOO SSSHHH

CAPTURE THEM, YOU BAND OF NINCOMPOOPS!

QUICK! WHILE THEY'RE NO LONGER PAYING ATTENTION TO ME!

⸴HMMPF!⸵

CRASH

NO! DON'T TOUCH THAT!

WRETCH! I'LL TURN YOU TO ASHES!

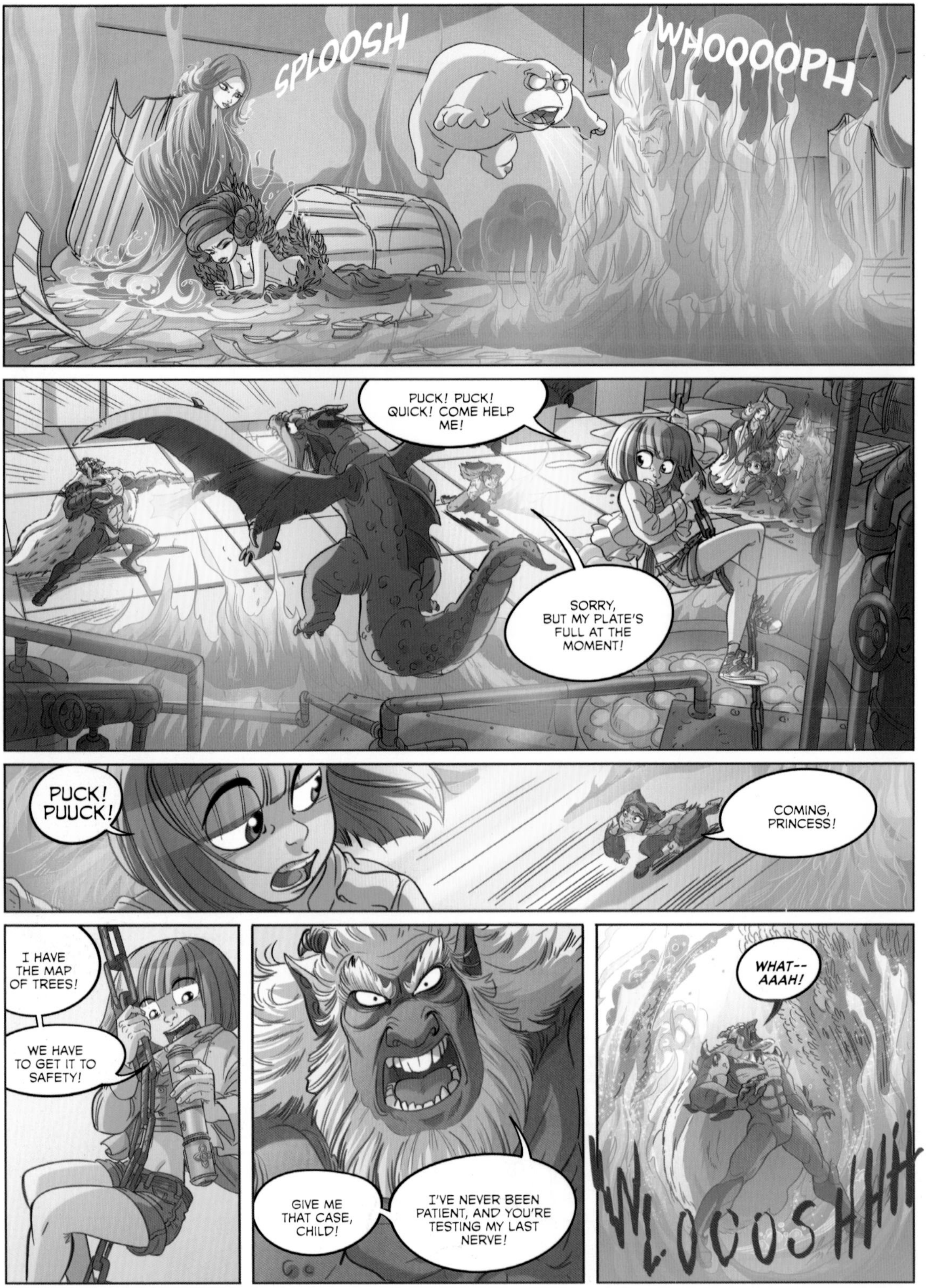
SPLOOSH
WHOOOOPH
PUCK! PUCK! QUICK! COME HELP ME!
SORRY, BUT MY PLATE'S FULL AT THE MOMENT!
PUCK! PUUCK!
COMING, PRINCESS!
I HAVE THE MAP OF TREES!
WE HAVE TO GET IT TO SAFETY!
GIVE ME THAT CASE, CHILD!
I'VE NEVER BEEN PATIENT, AND YOU'RE TESTING MY LAST NERVE!
WHAT-- AAAH!
WLOOOSHHH

AAAAH! HELP!

HELP US! SAVE US!

NO! NOT WATER! IT'S HORRIBLE!

≟BLUB≟ ≟BLURB!≟

≟BLAORB!≟ ≟BLORD!≟

≟AARGLARB!≟

IT'S NO USE THRASHING AROUND SO, LACKORS!

YOU KNOW BETTER THAN ANYONE THAT WHAT THE FOUR OF US DO TOGETHER IS INDESTRUCTIBLE!

GOOD JOB, LEO!

SO, LITTLE FAIRY OF MY DREAMS, ALL BETTER?

≟WHEW!≟ AMANITE! THAT DIRTY, LITTLE... WHERE IS SHE?

DISAPPEARED DURING THE BATTLE!

HOW WILL WE GET RID OF THE EGGS AND THAT POTION NOW? WE CERTAINLY CAN'T LEAVE THEM HERE!

NO, BUT WE CAN ALWAYS CHANGE THE COURSE OF THINGS!

THROW THIS FLOWER INTO THE CAULDRON, NINA!

THE POTION WILL BE RADICALLY CHANGED, TRUST ME!

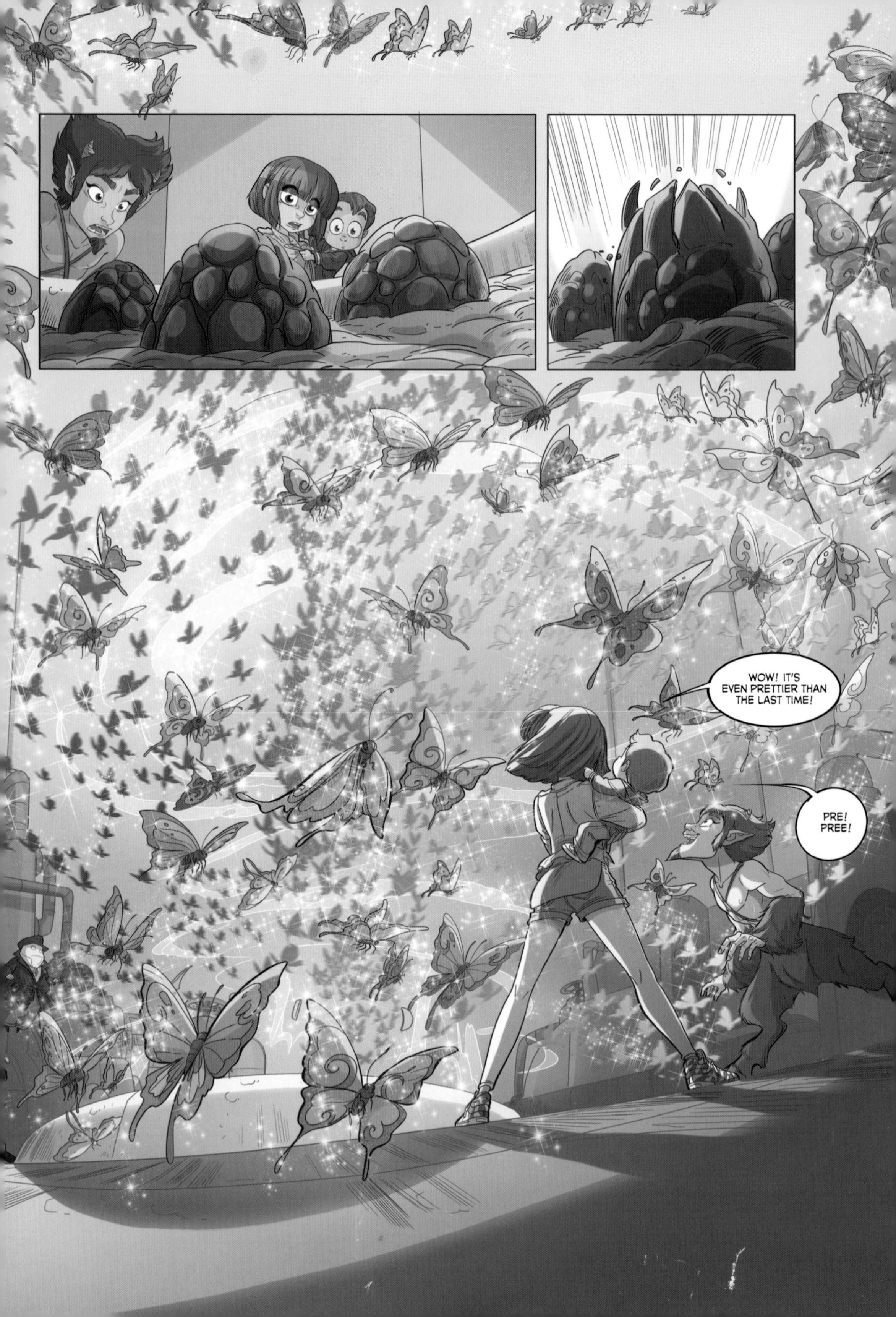

WOW! IT'S EVEN PRETTIER THAN THE LAST TIME!
PRE! PREE!

LEO! YOU'RE MY LITTLE LEO AGAIN!

N'NA! N'NA! TEDDY! TEDDY!

I'M SO HAPPY TO FIND YOU LIKE YOU WERE BEFORE!

HEE HEE HEE!

?

OH! OBERON AND TITIANIA!

YOUR MAJESTIES!

THANK YOU, NINA, FOR ALL THAT YOU'VE DONE THIS NIGHT!

BRAVO, SYBIL! YOU ACCOMPLISHED YOUR MISSIONS VERY WELL...

...EVEN THOUGH YOU AND PUCK HID MANY SERIOUS THINGS FROM ME!

BUT WHAT HAPPENED TO LEO?

WHY DOES HE CHANGE INTO A DRAGON?

IT'S QUITE SIMPLE, NINA. WHAT I'M GOING TO TELL YOU MUST REMAIN A SECRET BETWEEN US.

A SECRET THAT NEITHER YOUR PARENTS NOR YOUR BEST FRIEND'S MUST EVER LEARN.

I PROMISE, YOUR MAJESTY!

ELSA IS ONE OF OUR MANY DAUGHTERS! BUT ONE DAY, IN A FOREST, SHE MET YOUR FATHER, WHO WAS WORKING A STORY FOR HIS NEWSPAPER...

SHE WOULDN'T LEAVE HIM, EVEN THOUGH SHE KNEW THAT SHE COULD NO LONGER RETURN TO OUR WORLD.

HER FAIRY MEMORY FADED AWAY, AND SHE ADOPTED THE LIFE OF A HUMAN. THERE, NOW YOU KNOW EVERYTHING!

AS FOR YOU, LACKORS, YOU'LL GO BACK INTO THE EXILE YOU SHOULD HAVE NEVER LEFT!

AND UNDER CLOSE SURVEILLANCE!

WHERE-- WHERE DID THEY GO?

LACKORS WAS SENT TO AN ISLAND BETWEEN THE WORLD OF MEN AND OURS, FROM WHICH NO SPELL WILL REMOVE HIM. AND THE FOUR ELEMENTS HAVE REJOINED THEIR WORLD.

FINALLY, MRS. IBBINS IS ONCE AGAIN BACK HOME WITH NO MEMORY OF HER ADVENTURE.

WE MUST LEAVE YOU NOW, NINA.

BUT WE'LL SEE EACH OTHER AGAIN SOON! WE'RE PROUD OF YOU!

SEE YOU SOON-- GRANDMOTHER! GOODBYE, GRANDFATHER!

I HAVE TO LEAVE, TOO, GIRLS! BUT THE THREE OF US MAKE A HECKUVA TEAM!

SEE YOU SOON, PUCK!

GOODBYE, GOAT FEET! HEE HEE HEE!

SO NOW WE JUST HAVE TO GO HOME!

POOR LEO! ALL THIS FUSS PUT HIM TO SLEEP!

WHAT A NIGHT! I'LL BE COMPLETELY BURNED OUT TOMORROW AT SCHOOL.

DON'T WORRY! I HAVE A LITTLE RAPID-SLEEP SPELL THAT'S VERY REFRESHING!

46

YOU'RE NOT GOING TO THE OFFICE TODAY, MOM?

NO, I TOOK THE DAY OFF. I'M GOING TO LOOK AFTER LEO AND STRAIGHTEN UP THE HOUSE. DON'T BE TOO LONG COMING HOME.

DON'T FORGET WE HAVE A SKYPE DATE WITH YOUR DAD!

I WOULDN'T MISS IT FOR ANYTHING IN THE WORLD! SEE YOU TONIGHT, MOM!

AFTER A VERY, VERY LONG DAY OF CLASSES...

WHAT'S GOING ON, NINA? DID YOU AND ANTOINE HAVE A FIGHT?

≥PFF!≤ IT'S NOT THAT SIMPLE, JEANNE...

YOU SHOULD TALK TO HIM. IT CAN'T BE OVER BETWEEN THE TWO OF YOU!

YOU THINK SO? YES, MAYBE I'LL TELL HIM THAT...

NINA! JEANNE!

YOU CAN FINISH YOUR CHAT OUTSIDE!

YOU CAN GO NOW! SEE YOU TOMORROW!

ANTOINE! HEY, ANTOINE! WAIT UP!

HMM? OH, NINA!

I WANTED TO TELL YOU ABOUT YESTERDAY EVENING THAT-- I'M SORRY!

I DIDN'T MEAN TO HURT YOUR FEELINGS.

HUH? OH, YEAH, ABOUT THAT...

DON'T WORRY, IT'S OKAY! YOU KNOW, LAURIE IS REALLY NICE! WE HAVE A GOOD TIME TOGETHER!

AH YES-- LAURIE.

AND, ON SATURDAY WE'RE GOING HORSE-RIDING TOGETHER! THAT'S COOL, ISN'T IT?

UH-- YES, YES, THAT'S COOL.

ANTOINE!

ARE YOU COMING? YOU PROMISED TO WALK ME HOME!

I'M COMING, PRETTY GIRL! HA HA HA!

BYE, NINA!

OH, WELL! EITHER LAURIE HAS A CRAZY CHARM OR YOUR ANTOINE IS COMPLETELY IDIOTIC!

YES, HE'S NOT THE SAME ANY- MORE.

HE'LL COME AROUND ONCE HE SEES WHO LAURIE REALLY IS. SEE YOU TOMORROW, NINA!

YES, FOR SURE-- SEE YOU TOMORROW, JEANNE!

AND THANKS FOR BEING MY FRIEND!

YOU'RE WELCOME, GIRLY, IT'S MY PLEASURE!

AMANITE! IT WAS YOU! YOU CAST A SPELL ON ANTOINE SO HE'D BE SMITTEN WITH LAURIE! THAT'S WHY HE'S NO LONGER THE SAME!

SO WHAT? LAURIE WAS UNHAPPY, AND I ADORE LOVE STORIES WITH A HAPPY ENDING! SEE YOU SOON, DARLING!

ARE YOU CRYING?

OH--

AND POOF! A SMALL, MAGICAL PUFF THAT BLOWS AWAY TEARS AND BRINGS SMILES TO LIFE!

THANKS, SYBIL...

...MY LIFE WOULD BE A LOT MORE NORMAL WITHOUT YOU!

MAYBE! BUT YOU'D BE SO BORED! HA HA HA!

HA HA HA!

The End

48